'90s Island

'90s Island

A Novella by Marty Beckerman

INFECTED PRESS   NEW YORK, NEW YORK

Cover design by Danny Hellman

ISBN-10: 0-9700629-5-8
ISBN-13: 978-0-9700629-5-6

"The perfect world was a dream that your primitive cerebrum kept trying to wake up from. Which is why the Matrix was redesigned to this, the peak of your civilization."

—Agent Smith, *The Matrix* (1999)

I:
It's the End of the World as We Know It

1.

The 1960s were the happiest time of my father's life, and not simply because of the free love and cheap drugs. The decade represented something more to him: an ideal of civic passion, living completely in the moment, throwing off the shackles of a corrupt system...and creating some killer music in the process.

But when the '60s ended, Dad couldn't let them go. I don't just mean that he bought Clapton deluxe box sets or paid a fortune to see Rolling Stones concerts like a normal baby boomer. While his friends entered law school, medical school and business school, my father continued to drop acid, listen to sitar records and wear tie-dye. Not so flattering on his pot-bellied, middle-aged figure.

Mom basically raised us—my twin brother Zack and me—on her own. Dad spent his time camping out in front of the White House to protest

Ronald Reagan's policies, which sought to recreate the 1950s. (Well, an idealized version of the '50s. A seductively sanitized version.)

"Get a job, hippie," sneered the briefcase-carrying, Brooks Brothers-clad yuppies who could hardly believe the walking anachronism. Their conservative predecessors in the '60s told Dad to "get a job and a haircut," but he had no hair left.

Everybody needs a golden age. All that glitters is old.

2.

Our parents' marriage was disintegrating, but—at age five—Zack and I didn't comprehend that. We heard them arguing (*"Will you stop smoking that crap around the children?"*), but figured they were pretend-fighting like the two of us did when we played Ninja Turtles.

Until one night, while we slept in matching Ghostbusters pajamas, Dad sneaked to his Volkswagen bus—parked in front of our Northwest Washington, D.C., home—and drove off toward a California commune where he could reenact the Summer of Love with his fellow '60s burnouts.

After she'd finished crying her eyes out, Mom explained to Zack and me that most adults have something called *nostalgia*, which makes them want to be kids again ("Well, not *kids*, exactly, a little older") but Dad had *too much*, so much it made him sick. I promised myself, in all my kindergartner wisdom, that I'd never be like him. And so I never was. The end.

Psych. As if. Not.

3.

The rock stars Dad idolized were all fat, wrinkled and gray—or dead—but Kurt Cobain was a hero for *us*, a hero in the here and now. On November 13, 1993, Nirvana played Bender Arena at American University, a short walk from our house. Clever beyond his nine years, Zack hatched a scheme to get us inside.

The loading dock, which he'd scoped out the previous weekend, had no security presence until a couple hours before an evening concert, but the crew began wheeling instruments and technical equipment from the tour bus around noon. Zack and I hid behind amplifier stacks until the coast was clear, and then ducked into a backstage bathroom. We stayed there for half a day.

(At one point Dave Grohl took a dump in the next stall over. Let's just say he had a gift for screaming at top volume long before the Foo Fighters.)

We got to watch Nirvana with full backstage access. They covered the hits, from "Smells Like Teen Spirit" to "Come as You Are" to "Heart-Shaped Box," and then finished with seven minutes of disharmonious feedback, probably so Kurt felt less like a sellout for covering the hits.

He lifted his guitar to smash it and saw us peeking out from behind the black drapes.

"Freshmen look younger every year..." Kurt smirked. "Early graduation present."

He slid the guitar across the stage in our direction, like the way you'd give a foul ball to kids at an MLB game. Instantly our most cherished possession; instantly our most cherished memory.

4.

Neither of us could *play* the guitar, unfortunately, no matter how many instructors Mom paid to impart chords or keys or scales. Despite this handicap, music became my life.

As a preteen I spent every day at Georgetown Gutter, an independent record store and eccentric freak hangout. (Watch the film *Empire Records* for visuals; we even had a chick with a shaved head.) It's where I discovered *Dookie, Smash, Odelay, Siamese Dream, 40 Oz. to Freedom, The Downward Spiral, OK Computer, Check Your Head, Fashion Nugget, Pinkerton, Jagged Little Pill* (a work of genius, deal with it), *Blood Sugar Sex Magick* (back when Red Hot Chili Peppers songs had some actual variety) and countless other essential albums.

I'd spend hours upon hours rearranging CDs in my binder—alphabetically, by genre, by color—after I added a new one to the collection. Sometimes I felt like I'd die of a heart attack from jumping around my bedroom with the Aiwa stereo on full blast, but I kept dancing anyway.

As soon as I was old enough to get a job, I applied for a clerk position at the Gutter, which allowed me to hear the next week's alternative releases in advance. (No online streaming back then—music didn't *leak*—so you had to work at a record store or radio station.)

I wanted to discover as much new music as possible. Dad only listened to music from washed-up dinosaurs who hadn't mattered in twenty years; I embraced the cutting edge. *I was nothing like him...*

Yet.

5.

Today I still work at the same place. I've outlasted everyone else on the Gutter's staff, rising through the ranks to become head manager. A solid career trajectory—just in time for record stores to go extinct.

With so many customers browsing the racks, we used to exceed fire code capacity at any given moment. Now a couple folks walk through the door each day, usually confused senior citizens looking to replace their rainwater guards. ("But you're called Georgetown *Gutter*...")

No one cares that mp3s typically have an *eleventh* of CD audio quality. No one wants the clutter of liner notes and jewel boxes. Why pay $19.99 like you did *in* 1999? Twenty bucks for a CD...Jesus, nobody will pay twenty *cents* anymore.

"GOING OUTTA BUSINESS SALE," reads the banner over my head. "EVERYTHING DIES—NOW IT'S OUR TURN."

This place defined my adolescence. Now it defines my obsolescence.

6.

My Motorola SkyWord pager beeps. Its speaker burned out long, long ago and now releases a jarring electronic squawk. My girlfriend, Melanie, begs me daily to get a smartphone—but who needs change if old stuff is good enough? Why do I need to upload photos of my brunch to Instagram?

Zack's on my side. He has the exact same model of beeper (in similar run-down condition), which can receive and display a whole sentence. We were texting before it was cool.

"DREADING THIS," Zack presently transmits. "MEET IN 30?"

I lock up the shop and walk from Georgetown to Foggy Bottom, passing by embassies, churches, stone bridges and the Watergate. It's cold outside, but not *winter*. We had snow every December in the '90s, back when climate change was just a prediction—a problem for some far-off civilization—not a reality that melted ice caps, intensified hurricanes and made everyone feel a deep, steady, apocalyptic unease.

On my Sony Discman I listen to a mix CD, the original shuffle: 311's "All Mixed Up," the Wallflowers' "One Headlight," Marcy Playground's "Sex and Candy." But it cuts out midway through because skip protection and Mega Bass are hell on AA batteries.

Melanie exits the State Department. She's an aide to the deputy secretary; it's mind-numbing bureaucratic work but super-prestigious, and there's more of a future in her profession than mine. The faster the world changes, the *more* she's needed.

"Hi, sweetie..." She kisses me. "How did work go?"

"Oh, I think a buzzard *actually* flew over the store...you?"

"The usual. Another day, another international crisis."

"What's it now? Or top-top-*above*-top-secret again?"

"It's on CNN, MSNBC...the whole San Añorar situation?"

I have absolutely no idea what she's talking about. I stopped paying attention to the news after 9/11 made the world such a goddamned bummer all the time.

"All right, it's like this..." Melanie proceeds to explain without judgment of my ignorance; she enjoys playing expert. "The country's dictator, Julian Shango—you know, the guy with the mustache and golden Beretta pistol?—is facing imminent overthrow.

It's a mass movement, disorganized, without a clear leader. If Shango's fledgling nuclear program falls into the wrong hands...not like it's in the *right* hands now, but he's the devil we know..."

This geopolitics stuff always goes over my head—Melanie is so *smart*—but I nod along anyway.

"Shango's coming to D.C. tomorrow for emergency military funds, but State hasn't taken a position yet," she continues. "If we let him fall, the region might become unstable. If we support him and he *still* falls, we're in a bad negotiating position with the new government. There are no good options. We have an obvious interest in promoting democracy, but after Iraq..." She stops herself. "Enough realpolitik. Let's focus on the *happy* occasion!"

"You mean the worst occasion that's ever happened?"

"So melodramatic, Jake. It's a little birthday dinner."

"A *little* birthday?" I almost shriek. "That's like saying a little *cancer*."

"You're only as old as you feel..." She rolls her eyes at the cliché. "And maybe if you didn't dwell on the past so much, you *wouldn't* feel so old."

I've heard a million variations of this lecture. I usually tune it out, but I can't today.

"I'd rather dwell on the past," I say, "than on turning th...thir...thirrrrrrrrrr—"

7.

"HAPPY 30TH, HIND BROTHERS!" the icing on the candle-topped cake reads. Zack and I groan as the waiter brings it out.

"Make a wish, guys," Melanie chirps. "No wishing you were still twenty-nine."

"How are we three years older than Kurt lived to be?" I sigh.

"He used to seem like such an *adult*," Zack says.

"This is how you want to celebrate?" Melanie asks. "Come on, make your wishes!"

As Zack and I mutually blow out the candles, I wish that record stores were still vital community hubs. I wish that I still felt optimistic and carefree. I wish that the recession hadn't wiped out my generation's hope of a better tomorrow just as we were coming into real adulthood. (Upward mobility is a silly dream; a mortgage is a ridiculous fairy tale.) Young people were unemployed slackers by *choice* in the '90s; now it's because we don't have any choice.

"I wish people still read newspapers," Zack says. "Oh, I got laid off today."

"Jesus, man, I'm so sorry," I say. "How could they fire you on your birthday?"

"They didn't know..." Zack takes a gulp of his whiskey; we'd both ordered old-fashioneds. "It was only a matter of time anyway."

Zack started his journalism career at the high school paper; his investigative article on our vice principal embezzling from the cafeteria's budget won him the Excellence in Youth Reporting Award from the Society of Professional Journalists. The local alt-weekly gave Zack a regular column, his personal soapbox for exposing society's harsh truths.

But in recent years, he discovered a truth too harsh for him to accept: Journalism no longer *was* a career. Online media conglomerates now paid amateurs and interns next to nothing (or actual nothing) for aggregated/plagiarized sensationalist click-bait, TV episode recaps, photo listicles of kittens and "Sponsored Content" written on advertisers' behalf, unthinkable in a prior age of editorial ethics.

For guys like Zack, too pure for his own good, it meant waiting for the ax to fall.

"My boss told me, 'You're lucky, Hind, not all of us are young enough to change professions—I have to go down with the ship,'" Zack recounts. "He actually suggested I apply for a *government job.* 'The one enterprise that never goes bankrupt.'"

"If there's anything I can do to help..." Melanie offers. "I could pass your résumé around the State Department."

"*I'm supposed to be your fucking watchdog,*" Zack snaps. "Since when do journalists become members of the military-industrial civilian-killing baby-slaughtering fascist *complex*?"

Oh yeah, I should mention: Zack's emotional range is limited to indignation. He was always like this—going back to his political awakening at the 1996 Tibetan Freedom Concert—and he's probably spent more cumulative time listening to Rage Against the Machine than anyone else on earth. He even got arrested at the 1999 Seattle WTO riots for destruction of private and public property, which only solidified his adolescent guerilla glorification.

Not like it's bad to stand up for social justice, but there's a fine line between helpful benevolence and vainglorious zealotry. Zack's always a notch too intense; you can't bring him to house parties or weddings unless the theme is Dead Third-World Kids.

"Who even *wants* a public watchdog now?" Zack seethes with combustible rage. "Americans just want the latest gadget manufactured by Chinese preschoolers. Nobody protests; they merely click 'like' on useless Facebook petitions. You can't open eyes that are glued to a full-color touchscreen."

"Oh, that reminds me, Jake..." Melanie removes a gift-wrapped box from her purse.

I open it, expecting to find the Game Boy Color for which I'd asked. "Thanks, babe, I can't believe you tracked one down!"

To my dismay, I discover the new iPhone.

"It's to replace your horrible old pager," Melanie says. "It'll make your life so much easier. We're on the same service plan, so don't worry about the bill...my treat!"

Most of the time I keep a cool head, but suddenly I snap like Zack always does.

"I don't *want* my life to be easier," I say. "I don't need *change*, all right? Why can't you just let me be happy the way I am? The way I *was*?"

"I spent a week's paycheck on it..." Melanie looks crushed; I already feel terrible, but I can't take the outburst back. "You're *not* happy, Jake, can't you see that? You completely reject the present."

"I appreciate the gesture, all right?"

"I don't mean *my* present—*the* present. All your possessions are antiques; they belong in a museum, and your life *shouldn't* be one. When's the last time you even bought a new album?"

"Green Day's latest was okay. Sure, I preferred Billy Joe pre-guyliner, but—"

"A new album by a *new band*?"

"I don't like any new bands, duh."

"Do you know how difficult it is to love someone who hates everything?" She puts the unopened iPhone back in her purse and stands to leave.

"I love *you*, Mel," I say, debating whether to quote lyrics from Blink-182's "Don't Leave Me" or Lisa Loeb's "Stay."

"What's your girlfriend even doing here?" Zack says. "This dinner is *our* birthday tradition."

"That's sweet of you, Zack, really," Melanie says. "Way to make me feel like part of the family."

"You're not 'part of the family' until Jacob puts a ring on it," Zack says. "A ring some poor African child in a pitch-black mine with unsafe working conditions had to—"

"*Zack*," I say in utter mortification. "You're doing the opposite of helping."

"Actually, Jake, he's right..." Melanie's lip trembles. "I'm *not* one of you."

She wishes us a happy birthday and bursts into tears as she runs off.

8.

Zack and I don't feel much like celebrating, so we go to our house and drink ourselves into oblivion.

It made sense for us to move back home after Mom entered the assisted-living facility for her early-onset memory issues. Somebody had to take care of the place, and neither of us could afford rent elsewhere.

The same old posters (*Beavis & Butt-head*, "I WANT TO BELIEVE," the 1992 Olympic Dream Team) adorn my bedroom walls. Super Nintendo, Sega Genesis and N64 cartridges cover the floor: *GoldenEye 007*, *Donkey Kong Country*, *Battletoads*, *Sonic & Knuckles*, *F-Zero*, *Earthworm Jim*, *Kirby's Dream Land*, *Tomb Raider*, *Super Mario World*, *The Legend of Zelda: A Link to the Past*.

"We'll have to sell Kurt's guitar," I say, slumped on the carpet, a tumbler of Jim Beam Rye balanced precariously in my hand. "It's gotta be worth millions...what other choice is there?"

"Is that you talking, Jacob, or your killjoy girlfriend?" Zack says. "You can't just pawn our childhood."

"It really was happier in the '90s, right?" I spill alcohol on the floor. "We're not just romanticizing it 'cause we were kids?"

"It was *so much* happier," Zack says. "Thousands of guys our age hadn't died for Arab oil yet. Our biggest national crisis was an overabundance of boy bands and poseurs."

"Man, did we hate people who posed," I concur. "It's like, even the *colors* were happier in the '90s. All those old sitcoms—*Fresh Prince, NewsRadio, Dharma and Greg, Frasier, Home Improvement, Third Rock*—just have this blissful, insulated goofiness to them. We didn't watch gloomy crap like *The Walking Dead*. Why is everybody obsessed with zombies now?"

"Because everybody feels half-alive," Zack says. "Art reflects the times."

"I'd give anything for a time machine," I say. "Like, if I could travel to any era in history, I wouldn't meet Jesus or Shakespeare or Ben Franklin. I'd just go back and catch a Sublime concert before Brad Nowell overdosed."

"Wait..." Zack waves his hand; a flashbulb has popped inside his hyperactive brain. "Who says you need a time machine to go back to the '90s? What if we could *recreate* it?"

His face bears an urgent, laser-focused expression. He gets excited frequently, but I've rarely—if ever—seen him like *this*.

"You mean, hold a convention like *Star Trek* geeks?" I ask. "Or Civil War reenactors?"

"This wouldn't be for a quick, fleeting weekend," Zack says. "I'm talking about a *perfect replica*. The culture, the clothing, the cuisine, the catchphrases..."

"So you want to live in a commune like Dad?" I say. "Dude, I've heard a lot of drunk bullshit from you over the years, but this is—by far—the drunkest and bullshittiest."

"We buy a private island," Zack continues, undeterred. "Rollerblades, the primary, eco-friendly form of transportation. Pog and hacky-sack tournaments—not preemptive war and cutthroat capitalism—our competitive release. And people still read the newspaper each morning!"

"Do you *hear* how ludicrous you sound?"

Ludicrous, I silently admit, *yet wonderful*.

"Then why are you smiling so wide, Jacob?" Zack says. "You know we've got something here."

"Who in their right mind would follow us to some island in the middle of nowhere?"

"*Everybody*," Zack shouts. "All the '90s radio stations and '90s theme parties and '90s karaoke nights, all the sequels to '90s movies and rebooted '90s TV shows and reunited '90s bands...political polls show that Bill Clinton could win a third term, however unconstitutional, and Hillary's a lock. There's a collective, unprecedented *yearning* for that decade. And we're the ones who can fulfill it. We'll build a land of milk and honey, an oasis of rekindled dreams."

I know it's crazy, but Zack's schemes *have* worked before—hey, we got a Kurt Cobain instrument out of one—and, truth be told, this is everything I want in the world.

"Let's keep the guitar," I say, "and get the money from another source."

On my lime green iMac G3, I open Kickstarter, the crowdfunding site that allows musicians, filmmakers and entrepreneurs to beg their friends for money. I enter my Hotmail address (I'm heartbroken that Microsoft is automatically updating it to Outlook.com to sound more respectable) and create an account for our project: '90s ISLAND.

"This will be *revolutionary*." Zack waves a fist in the air. "The first *mass retro society*."

He sends the link to all of his media contacts. The night devolves into an ebullient alcoholic haze of whooping and delirious joy. For the first time in years, I feel young again. *Alive* again. Not a zombie.

9.

The hangover doesn't hit me...and then I lift my head off the pillow. Yep, there it is. I fight the nausea as I race to the bathroom to eject chunky filth from my body.

"What *happened* last night?" I moan between heaves, closing my eyes to hide the omnidirectional spinning.

I recall Melanie leaving the restaurant...Zack and me coming back to the house, and then...nothing. It's an opaque, amorphous blur.

"If you wanted to kill me," I ask God, pulling myself to my feet by some miracle and staggering back to the bedroom, "couldn't you have done it *before* I turned thirty?"

And then I notice an even greater miracle. My Hotmail inbox is filled with 175,000-plus messages from no-reply@kickstarter.com, all containing the subject line: "New Backer Alert!"

"Why am I getting spammed with all this shit?" I ask, mass deleting the emails without reading them. Moments later, the inbox fills back up with dozens, then hundreds, then *thousands* more of the exact same message.

"Are those the donations?" Zack stands in the doorway. "You've got *mail*?"

He rushes over to the computer; I can't handle sudden movements right now.

"Holy shit, we did it..." Zack opens the Kickstarter page—which shows our million-dollar total—and grabs my shoulders. "It's all about the Benjamins!" He laughs uncontrollably. "*Showwwwww meeeeeeee the monnnnnnnneeeeyyyyyyyyyyyyyy!*"

"That...actually happened?" I ask, beginning to remember.

Zack plugs "'90s Island" into Google News. We scored initial publicity from BuzzFeed (which loved the idea) and Gawker (which shat all over it). The story trickled down to other major outlets and got upvoted to the front page of Reddit. Zack might hate the way blogs lazily reword content from other blogs, but it worked beautifully for us.

"Put on your Sunday best," Zack says, opening the latest email (subject line: "MEDIA REQUEST") to hit my inbox. "We're going on national TV."

10.

A black sedan drives us to the broadcast network's D.C. bureau. (Miniature water bottle and tin of Altoids in each backseat cup holder...classy touch!)

We show our IDs to front-desk security. A producer escorts us upstairs, a makeup lady slathers us with foundation, and a sound technician runs microphone wires under our shirts.

In the green room I grab a lemon danish.

"Camera adds ten pounds," Zack says.

"You're lecturing me on *carb intake*?" I ask.

"This is our chance to sell '90s Island to an even wider audience, Jacob. We've gotta look as good as we sound."

"I don't know how to sound good on TV."

"Just smile and stay positive. If we nail this interview—low-hanging fruit—we'll have enough cash to buy any island on earth and live comfortably for the rest of our lives."

"Not Australia," I say. "I don't think it's for sale."

Zack sighs. "Marx had Engels...I have you."

The producer walks us to the set, which is bustling with activity between segments. I shiver from nervousness and because the soundstage is kept at meat-locker temperatures to protect the lighting gels. The anchorwoman, a brunette in her late thirties or maybe early forties—who looks even better in person than she does on the screen—greets us as we sit down on the couch.

"Very cool idea, guys," she says. "No time to rehearse, but I'll ask you about where it came from, where it's going...all that good stuff."

"Fantastic," Zack says, turning on the charm.

As the commercial break ends, the director counts down ("7...6...5...4..."), mouthing the last few numbers like in *Wayne's World*. I'm hyper-aware of my breathing and heartbeat.

"Welcome back," the anchorwoman says into the camera. "Recapping our top story, the U.S. will *not* provide foreign aid to San Añorar, despite President Julian Shango's appeals for it to soothe ongoing political strife. The State Department has urged caution and restraint on both sides. Making things even more delicate, San Añorar's military could soon finish construction of a nuclear warhead. We'll keep you updated as developments occur."

A camera pans over to Zack and me. I resist the infantile urge to wave or make a silly face.

"A modest proposal has received an extreme response," the anchorwoman says in a higher octave, instantly changing from sober to lighthearted topics. "Two brothers, Jake and Zack Hind, set up a Kickstarter fundraising page for ''90s Island,' a private colony devoted to the long-gone decade. Overnight, they received more than a *million dollars* from micro-donors throughout the country. A Powerball lottery winner their age is now promising to pitch in. Guys, I have to ask: Where did you *get* this idea?"

"We were hammered out of our minds," I blurt, "so I guess we got it at the liquor store."

"Yes, we'd had a few celebratory drinks," Zack intercedes, shooting me a furious glare and then flashing a smile to the camera. "But we're 100 percent serious, 100 percent committed. This place is *going* to exist, and it'll be heaven on earth."

He's rescued the interview from my ineptitude. He could be a politician. An unstoppable politician.

"Why the '90s?" the anchorwoman asks. "A decade ago, my friends and I were celebrating the '80s revival—jeez, *those* were the days—but nobody formed an expatriate society over it."

"The '90s were the exact, idyllic opposite of everything wrong with the world today," Zack says, hypnotically even-toned. "Who isn't sick of economic turmoil, military conflict, bleakness, cynicism and gritty Hollywood reboots? The '90s were joyous, playful, creative, uplifting and never should've ended. That's not just our opinion; it's an entire *generation's* opinion. A song titled 'Why Don't You Get a Job?' was a massive hit, not a question that millions of millennials frantically ask into their mirrors. Modern society has nothing to offer us, so we'll create a new one. '90s Island: *come as you are; stay as you were.*"

"If somebody breaks the time-traveling illusion—say, wears a Justin Bieber shirt—will they be punished? Solitary confinement with 'Who Let the Dogs Out?' playing on loop?"

"You make it sound like Orwell's *Nineteen Eighty-Four*." Zack laughs. "We're all about nineteen *ninety*-four. This will be an open, welcoming community for everyone who loves '90s culture, fashion, movies, games..."

"Music," I add, voice cracking.

"And music, of course," Zack says. "There might be some bylaws so everyone can live together peaceably—don't steal, don't kill, the usual social-contract clauses—but first we need more Kickstarter pledges to get the ball rolling and live *la vida loca*."

"Jake, your brother seems convinced this idea can work," the anchorwoman says. "People would have to leave behind everything: their jobs, their homes, their loved ones..."

"We'll have plenty of jobs there," I say. "And families are welcome."

"Yes, but do you agree this has a realistic chance of succeeding?"

"It's..." I feel the weight of the world on my shoulders; I *want* it to succeed, but I've never had Zack's certainty—so I choose to trust his outward enthusiasm over my inward doubts. "Absolutely. Who says you can't go home again?"

"On that note, Jake, Zack, thanks so much for joining us." The anchorwoman smiles; her teeth are impossibly white. "Good luck on your voyage back to the future."

"I think you mean *forward* to the *past*," Zack says, beaming.

"Allllrighty then." She winks. "That's a '90s saying, right?"

"We hella said it," I ejaculate. "Hellllllllllllllllla!"

The camera pans away. We're off-air. God, I'm an idiot.

11.

"Zack, you sounded *amazing*," I tell my brother as we exit the building. "I hope the VCR recorded it OK."

Although I expected the same black sedan to pick us up, a limousine driver holds a sign marked "HIND." We step inside, figuring the network dispatched a different vehicle. But the network had absolutely nothing to do with this, despite the limo's TV being tuned to it.

"Gentlemen, I congratulate you," says Julian Shango. "And I extend an invitation."

My brain can hardly process what my eyes are seeing. I might not follow politics like Zack and Melanie do, but it's surreal to sit across from a notorious twentieth-century icon.

"You believe I am a madman, yes?" Shango says with unflinching eye contact. "Hell-bent on nuclear destruction? With the propaganda spewed on your news outlets, how could you not?"

I already know what's coming before it does. "Our corrupt *corporate* news outlets with their profit-motive agendas," Zack says, not missing a beat. "Sir, I have so many T-shirts with your face...it's such an honor to meet you in person."

"Uh, Zack," I whisper, "I don't know much about foreign affairs, but isn't this guy an evil dictator?"

"You're so naïve," Zack says. "Comrade Julian has had to make difficult choices in the face of imperialist aggression, but he's done it all for the good of his citizenry. Who, by the way, enjoy better educational and medical standards than we do in our plutocratic kleptocracy."

"Oh...that's pretty solid, I guess?"

"Yes. *Yes.* Zackary, is it?" Shango says. "You *understand.*"

"*El Jefe,*" Zack says, "what 'invitation' do you have for us?"

"You boys need a habitable island, and I need money to quell a coup d'état," Shango says. "It's only logical, considering our mutual interests, that we strike a deal. In exchange for the pledges you've raised, I offer you San Añorar's southern coast—luxury hotels, entertainment facilities, miles of pristine beaches—and a lifetime of food, water, health care, security."

"In my wildest dreams," Zack says, "I couldn't imagine a greater bargain. What do you think, Jacob?"

"I...I..."

I have to admit: It's an incredible deal, enough to make my pulse race with excitement and adrenaline. I've always hated change, but this is changing *away* from change. If there's even a 1 percent chance we can make it happen...

"Yeah, I'm in."

"Excellent," Shango says. "Zackary, I knew I liked your sibling, 'evil dictator' prejudice aside."

"Let's pack our things..." Zack puts his arm around my shoulders, a more brotherly gesture than we've exchanged in ages. "We have a utopia to create."

12.

I stand on the terrazzo floor of the two-story limestone State Department lobby. This is as far as I'm allowed inside Melanie's workplace without a security clearance.

"Jake, I *cannot* talk right now," she says. "The situation in San Añorar is *extremely unstable*. If you came to discuss last night's dinner, can it please wait until—"

"Actually I came to talk about San Añorar," I say. "We're *moving* there!"

She stares at me blankly. "Is this some kind of joke I'm not getting?"

"*'90s Island*...you, uh, didn't read about it on the Internet today?"

"Jake..." She rubs her eyes. "What on earth are you blabbering about?"

I give her the rundown: Kickstarter, the TV appearance, Shango's offer.

"For God's sake," she says. "How drunk *were* you and Zack?"

"Super, super drunk," I say. "But we're on the verge of making this *happen*. We have the cash, the location, the homesteaders...all I need is you."

"Need me to *what*?"

"To come with me."

"Are you insane, Jake? Are we having this conversation—about wiring funds to a rogue power, a violation of the Trading with the Enemy Act—*inside the State Department lobby*?"

"Um..." I say. "Yes?"

"Look, I'm going to be very clear, because this has been a long time coming. You are suffering from a nostalgia-induced mental breakdown, just like your father did. You and Zack have...I don't know what to call it...a *genetic psychiatric issue* with idealizing days gone by. I want to build a future together, but that's impossible if you're trying to *re*build the past."

"The past was so much *better*, Mel, don't you remember?"

"You're forgetting Columbine, Rwanda, Kosovo, Oklahoma City, *Batman and Robin*..."

"Actually I prefer Clooney to Bale," I confess. "What's wrong with Day-Glo corniness? Bring on the Bat Nipples!"

She kisses me on the forehead. "Jake, I would follow you anywhere...but I won't—I can't—follow you any*when*."

"This is everything I want...I can't choose between *it* and us."

She shakes her head and turns. "Then you already have."

Unlike me every day of my life, Melanie doesn't look back.

II:
Welcome to Paradise

13.

Zack proves a phenomenally adept manager of the logistics. Or maybe it's just phenomenal what you can accomplish with millions of dollars—from purchasing countless vintage items off eBay (the most decadent: a $10,000 gallon of McJordan barbeque sauce) to chartering a fleet of cruise ships for the San Añorar-bound exodus.

It hurts to say goodbye to Mom at the assisted-living facility. I can't shake the feeling that we're abandoning her, but the sale of the house will provide her with long-term care. And that's more than Zack and I could have done *without* '90s Island, so aren't we being faithful sons?

I keep wishing that Melanie would change her mind. Leaving her is like chopping out my own heart. Problem is, the last decade didn't go *wrong* for her like it did for everyone else. But if '90s Island works—if Zack and I make it the promised land that we know it can be—then she'll understand.

Then she'll believe. In it. In *me*.

14.

News helicopters circle overhead, filming our nautical departure. We've become the biggest story in the world: a significant chunk of Generation Y leaving our physical homeland for our *spiritual* homeland.

Some Kickstarter backers complained that we chose a nondemocratic nation for our location, but most understand that we'll have total political autonomy. The U.S. government tried to stop us with various injunctions, but we haven't given Shango a dime yet. And we're not taking cash out of the country, which could warrant Coast Guard action.

On the advice of our lawyers—recent J.D.s who can't find jobs to pay off their crippling loans—we opened a Swiss bank account, from which we can wire the money to San Añorar's treasury upon our arrival. (Zack rants for hours about how the economic sanctions are designed to starve San Añorari children as a form of political blackmail against Shango. I'm not sure I disagree.)

The last of the passengers file onboard. The flagship's horn blows; its engine hums. Standing on the bridge, I feel the vibrations in my bones as we pull away from the harbor.

This is real. This is happening. This is *us*.

"We're the kings of the world," Zack says.

"Yeah, dude," I say. "We're going to make history."

"No, Jacob," Zack says. "We're going to unmake it."

15.

We arrive after a couple days at sea. White sand and palm-tree dew glimmer in the sunshine. I've never seen turquoise water up close—just the aquamarine of the East Coast—and it's even more gorgeous than in travel brochures (another antiquated victim of the Internet). I haven't even set foot on the island yet, but I could stay here forever.

As our ships dock at the pier, my brother grabs the intercom.

"Citizens of '90s Island, welcome home," Zack says. "And welcome to the dawn of a new age. One that will never age. One that will always, *always* be gettin' jiggy with it."

The passengers clap thunderously, and they cheer throughout disembarkation.

"Welcome, welcome!" Shango says, meeting us at the pier, flanked by armed security guards, his signature gold-plated Beretta at his hip. "You are such an incredible sight."

"*San Añorar* is the incredible sight," Zack says, both diplomatic and sincere. "I want to kiss the ground like a goddamned Jew landing at Ben Gurion Airport."

"Everything has been prepared to your specifications..." Shango gestures toward the seemingly endless row of beachfront resort complexes separated by lush foliage and extravagant amenities. "Only the best for my friends."

"Let's party," Zack says.

"Like it's 1999?" I say.

"Like it always will be."

16.

The first step in recreating the '90s: get everybody to look the part. Zack and I report to fashion central, which we've dubbed MORPHIN' TIME, for a proper makeover. Guys can choose between two hairstyles: frosted tips ("The Justin Timberlake") or curtains

("The Jonathan Taylor Thomas"). Female '90s Island citizens universally receive "The Rachel," Jennifer Aniston's greatest contribution to humanity. Is anything sexier?

The stylist assigned to Zack and me can't believe that she has *the* Hind brothers as clients, as if we were royalty like Prince William and Prince Harry (who chose the Timberlake and the JTT, respectively).

"Thank you, *thank you*," she says with undisguised reverence. "You guys are *heroes*."

"We just had the idea for this place," Zack says in response to her borderline-worshipful adulation. "It wouldn't be real without you."

His false modesty could fool anyone who hadn't known him since the womb. And I'm not exactly feeling humble myself, considering the week's momentous achievements. How did I live without *confidence* for all of the aughts? How did I exist in such a calcified state of half-slumber?

The stylist conditions my hair before applying bleach and peroxide. (The sharp chemical scent brings me way, *way* back during my thirty minutes under a heating dome with a shower cap on.) She adds toner to ensure that my frosted tips come out yellow, not orange, and then spikes 'em with L.A. Looks Mega Hold Styling Gel.

My frosted tips. I'm not sure whether to laugh or cry with nostalgic joy; I can't stop looking in the mirror. Neither can Zack, whose locks turn out even *more* finger-in-socket white.

We proceed to the Slim Fit Collection Bin, depositing our snug modern clothes—skinny jeans, tailored shirts, boxer briefs—and picking replacements from a warehouse of vintage apparel: comically saggy JNCOs and high-riding elastic-waistband denim, plaid flannel and Hawaiian button-downs, Adidas track jackets, MC Hammer-style parachute pants, skateboard-logo T-shirts (Thrasher, Hook-Ups, Alien Workshop), assorted graphic Ts (Mossimo, No Fear, Big Dogs, Looney Tunes gangstas), FUBU sweatshirts and Tommy Hilfiger everything.

I want to select more of these outfits than I can physically carry—*so much beautiful neon*—but I limit myself to the standard citizen's textile ration of fifteen pounds, an average laundry bag's weight. (Could I abuse my executive privilege as a '90s Island cofounder? Sure, if this were *Animal Farm*, but it's more like *Camp Nowhere*.)

We complete our new wardrobes with old-school kicks—a difficult choice between Doc Martens,

Reebok Pumps, Skechers, Vans, Airwalks, Hush Puppies, Air Jordans and L.A. Lites that blink red with every step—and bodacious accessories: puka-shell necklaces, bucket hats, terry-cloth wristbands, Oakley sunglasses, studded, overlong belts, chain wallets, slap bracelets.

It's like no time has passed.

It's like a nightmare is over.

It's like a dream has begun.

17.

For our opening ceremony, San Añorar's southern coastline becomes one massive rave illuminated by stroboscopic lasers, UV black lights and phosphorescent glow-sticks. Freak dancing everywhere, just like high school prom, albeit with translucent mesh instead of tuxes and gowns.

And then I see the girl of my '90s dreams: zebra-striped hoop earrings, shredded black Riot Grrrl babydoll, silver vinyl pants and florescent pink boots. Even her nose ring turns me on. As much as I miss Melanie, I become torturously aware of my new single status. I'm terrified to introduce myself. (Christ, this *is* like high school.) But Zack notices me checking her out and forces my hand.

"Zack Hind here..." He approaches the girl with inimitable magnetism. "Perhaps you've heard of me and my brother Jacob? Who, FYI, is crushing *hard* on you."

"Sorry for the disturbance," I say. "This is just a big misunderst—"

"You're cute..." She gives me a once-over and then opens an Altoids tin with multicolored tabs inside. "Want some X?"

"Uh..." I'm flabbergasted. "Like ecs*tasy*?"

Zack reaches into the tin. "You in, bro?"

I've never touched it—only pot—and I'm hesitant to ingest a new chemical beyond college. But our rave's hedonic atmosphere compels me; I shock myself by popping a baby blue tab imprinted with a smiley face.

"I'll leave you two alone..." Zack slaps my back, smirking with bemused pride, and whispers in my ear, "You'll never want to fuck sober again."

The girl, named Evangeline, basically walked right out of the movie *Hackers*. She began coding with Apple's HyperCard on a Power Mac in elementary school, and could've worked for any technology company in the world. Bolstering their bottom lines, however, appealed to her less than breaching their firewalls and leaking evidence of their malfeasance to the world.

"Because fuck the system, right, Hind?" Evangeline concludes her story. "I'll take the ending of *Fight Club* over a mid-six-figure salary at some bullshit transnational corporation."

We've been talking for half an hour, and—*enraptured* by her—I've completely forgotten about the ecstasy...until the electronica pulsating from omnipresent speakers (Chemical Brothers, Prodigy, Aqua, Real McCoy) acquires an effervescence that cuts through my brain like a buzz saw. Fireworks of golden warmth burst through my body, ejecting from my fingertips—like Jubilee from the *X-Men* cartoon— in vibrant prismatic colors that I wasn't aware existed.

"So *that's* why people listen to techno," I realize at long last. "*Drugs!*"

Dancing with Evangeline is like infinite, incandescent orgasm. She licks my neck and nibbles my earlobes; I shudder with pleasure. My entire body has become an erogenous zone. When Nine Inch Nails' "Closer" plays, Trent Reznor's words could be my own.

"I'd ask 'your place or mine?'" she says. "But *this whole place* is your place."

18.

Do I feel guilty in the morning? No, because I can't feel anything at all. My neurotransmitters are fried to a crisp, my serotonin reserves evaporated, my energy gone.

Zack sends a message to my SkyWord pager: "BREAKFAST, MR. LOVERMAN?"

(We switched our devices to Shango's cellular network because U.S.-based telecommunications companies don't provide service to San Añorar. Good riddance, AT&T.)

I'm surprised that the beeper's awful squawk doesn't awaken Evangeline, but she took more X than I did. I leave her sleeping naked in bed, spritz myself with CK One, the official scent of '90s Island, and meet Zack in the cafeteria, which—in addition to omelets, pancakes, sausage links and other fresh options—is stocked with all the '90s foodstuffs that money can buy: PB Crisps, Doritos 3D chips, Oreo O's, Shark Bites, Butterfinger BB's, Cheetos Paws, Gummi Savers, Berry Berry Kix, Keebler Fudge Magic Middles, Soda Licious Fruit Snacks, Ninja Turtles Cereal and Hostess Ninja Turtles Pies ("FILLED WITH VANILLA PUDDIN' POWER").

As if that weren't enough to induce diabetes, liquid options include Josta, Jolt, Surge, Crystal Pepsi, Hi-C Ecto-Cooler, Squeeze-Its, Fruitopia, Orbitz (those floating tapioca globules are so gross, yet so great) and Capri Sun's original high-fructose formula. Mom used to pack this stuff in our Power Rangers lunch boxes—along with turkey sandwiches and sliced apples for actual nutrition—back when she was capable of linear thought. It's a blast from the culinary past, and I pile my plastic tray high.

"You're sure this stuff is still edible?" I ask Zack, opening a package of Dunkaroos from 1996. (We could've bought unexpired ones at any grocery store—they're not discontinued like most of the aforementioned items—but he demanded 100 percent authenticity.)

"If eating it kills us," Zack says, "I can't imagine a better way to die."

I take a trepidatious bite. It's stale but decent, and a swish of Jolt softens the texture...then *jolts* me out of my post-narcotic stupor with enough caffeine to wake the dead.

"Dunkaroos are *da bomb*, yo," I say, tossing a handful into my face.

"All that and a bag of chips, beeyotch." Zack rips open the Doritos 3Ds.

"We're gonna get so fat..." I grin from ear to ear. "With an 'f,' not a 'ph.'"

The catchphrase-laden banter continues. Forget the drug; *this* is ecstasy.

19.

The south wing of Shango's palace, on the dividing line between our side of the island and his, becomes our City Hall. From the outside it looks like a prison—electrified fences, guard towers, watchdogs on the prowl—but inside it's opulent enough for Saddam Hussein or Donald Trump. With high-tech jail cells in the basement, it kinda *is* a prison.

Per our request, Shango has a marble statue of Kurt Cobain erected in the lobby. At its base, the guitar that Kurt gave Zack and me is encased in glass.

We spend hours on administrative duties. I organize playlists for the shortwave radio networks that beam '90s tunes 24/7. Zack creates a schedule for our local television station. (All TV sets must be CRT monitors with square aspect ratios, not rectangular flat-screens.) Today's lineup: *The X-Files, Full House, Who Wants to Be a Millionaire?, Buffy the Vampire Slayer, Gargoyles, Dawson's Creek, Xena: Warrior Princess, Lois and Clark: The New Adventures of*

Superman, Freaks and Geeks, Clarissa Explains It All, Malcolm in the Middle, Are You Afraid of the Dark?, Doug, In Living Color, Animaniacs, Tiny Toons Adventures and *The Simpsons* prior to season twelve, when it still deserved to call itself *The Simpsons*.

"This feels too much like working on vacation," Zack says, typing notes into his Palm Pilot and filing government documents into his Trapper-Keeper. "Let's *explore!*"

At the central boardwalk that forms the heart of '90s Island, our fellow citizens skateboard, Rollerblade and Razor-scoot from attraction to attraction. Tower Records, Borders Books & Music, Circuit City and Sam Goody might've gone out of business in the real world, but we've brought them back to life here. Want to watch a movie at home? There's no Netflix streaming, no Hulu, no Amazon Prime...just Blockbuster Video renting out classic VHS tapes in blue, white and yellow plastic cases. The newest "New Releases" are from 1999.

(Zack and I had some debate over whether to allow films from 2000. *Cast Away, Gladiator, Almost Famous, What Women Want, Erin Brockovich, Charlie's Angels, Miss Congeniality, O Brother, Where Art Thou?, Road Trip, Wonder Boys* and *Me, Myself & Irene* are essentially '90s movies with a pre-9/11 Hollywood aesthetic. But if we start fudging our own rules, Zack and I concluded, why did we even come here?)

Tickets at '90s Island's movie theater cost four bucks for a matinee and seven bucks otherwise, not *thirteen* like at modern megaplexes. No 3-D or IMAX or 48 fps surcharges either. The marquee damn near brings tears to my eyes, and I can't decide which classic I want to see first:

NOW PLAYING:

SPACE JAM	AMERICAN PIE
PULP FICTION	JURASSIC PARK
AUSTIN POWERS	THE SIXTH SENSE
DUMB & DUMBER	CLERKS
BRAVEHEART	INDEPENDENCE DAY
TOMMY BOY	CLUELESS
MEN IN BLACK	TERMINATOR 2
SAVING PRIVATE RYAN	HAPPY GILMORE
TOY STORY	ACE VENTURA

THERE'S SOMETHING ABOUT MARY

It was like a parallel universe, a *better* universe that should've existed all along. (A parallel universe where *The Matrix* didn't have any sequels.) Evangeline meets us for a showing of Tarantino's greatest. The non-digital picture feels warmer and more robust, like the visual equivalent of vinyl records.

Speaking of *Toy Story*, a recreated K·B Toys warehouses our generation's favorite childhood playthings. While Evangeline rediscovers her love for

Tamagotchis and Virtual Pets, Zack and I blast each other with Nerf weaponry and Super Soakers. (My single-canister Super Soaker 50—the original yellow, orange and green one—is no match for his backpack-style Super Soaker 300Z.) We get our hands gooey with Gak, Floam and Sticky Hands. We decapitate Crash Test Dummies. We save the earth with Captain Planet and the Planeteers. We were too old for Beanie Babies, Tickle Me Elmo and Furby, but younger '90s Island citizens play with those sentimental trinkets just like we're playing with ours.

And here's the thing: *We're not doing it ironically* like hipsters whose every action is a premeditated fashion statement. We're genuinely using our imaginations; we're remembering the thrill of playtime. Do kids today even *have* imaginations? Or just iPads and Galaxy tablets?

It's not like we grew up without electronics. The '90s Island arcade houses all the coin-operated greats: *Virtua Fighter*, *Killer Instinct*, *Cruis'n USA*, *Time Crisis*, *Area 51*, *The Simpsons: The Arcade Game* and *Mortal Kombat*, which Mom wouldn't let us play because of the excessive "FINISH HIM!" violence.

Are the graphics as impressive as those of modern video games? No...but the simplicity is part of the fun. You don't feel overwhelmed by immersive worlds; you just go from the left side of the screen to the right, and maybe punch somebody in the face.

My *Street Fighter II* skills are rusty; despite constant *hadoukens* and *shoryukens*, Zack destroys me with Guile's sonic booms and flash kicks. Evangeline ekes out a victory against him with Chun-Li's ability to bounce off the sides of the screen. (I remember masturbating to Chun-Li's 16-bit panties after pausing the SNES version. Not my proudest adolescent moment.)

A girl our age playing skee-ball wears a Barack Obama "HOPE" button pinned to her Old Navy Tech Vest.

"What the fuck is *this*?" Zack jabs the "O" with his index finger. "We have *fucking bylaws* here. Find a Clinton-Gore button. Or a Nader one...for his *'96* run, not 2000."

"Sorry, Mister H-H-Hind," the girl stammers. "Won't happen again."

His nod communicates: *better not happen again.*

"That was kinda harsh," I say. "People need time to adjust."

"We adjusted time," Zack says. "It wasn't a half-measure."

We leave the arcade and pass by the sports arena; it contains replicas of the *American Gladiators* set and the booby-trapped Aggro Crag mountain from *Nickelodeon Guts*. (No luck drafting Jordan, Pippen, Barkley or Johnson into our basketball league, but Rodman's down.)

My favorite attraction of all is the amphitheater, which hosts daily and nightly concerts. We've already managed to book Everclear, Smash Mouth, Sugar Ray, Eve 6, Third Eye Blind, Harvey Danger, Semisonic, Ace of Base, Hanson, the Verve Pipe, the Verve (no Pipe), Filter, Reel Big Fish, the Mighty Mighty Bosstones, the Cherry Poppin' Daddies and the Squirrel Nut Zippers (call it the Swing Revival *Revival*), and others who need the cash or newfound relevance.

I can't believe that I'm dancing to third-wave ska again without shame; it's been a guilty pleasure for so long—like fetishizing circus music—I could've sworn I was the only one who missed those horns and upstrokes...but thousands of rudies in black-and-white checkered outfits and cheap three-piece suits are presently dancing to Goldfinger's "Here in Your Bedroom."

I'm not alone here. *None of us will ever feel alone again.*

Even the pop music that I hated at the time for its pre-manufactured, mass-market, cookie-cutter soullessness—Backstreet Boys, 'N SYNC, Britney Spears—I now love just because it was *from* the time. (This goodwill doesn't extend to Limp Bizkit. Fred Durst is the only person banned from '90s Island; some historical artifacts are better left forgotten.)

Because hip-hop just wasn't my scene back then—in the '90s, middle-class white boys were expected to say "I listen to all music except country and rap," a pathetic sonic prejudice in retrospect—I didn't realize that rap fans have the *exact same* '90s nostalgia as alternative fans. So in addition to live performances from LL Cool J, Busta Rhymes, Diddy (now "Puff Daddy" again) and Snoop Lion (now "Snoop Doggy Dogg" again), the Tupac Shakur hologram from Coachella 2012 performs with a Notorious B.I.G. hologram. Enemies in life, collaborators in death. You could almost swear their ghostly, disembodied visages were the real thing.

Just like you could almost swear '90s Island was the real thing.

20.

Any doubts I had were now extinguished. Each initiative was more exciting than the last, even if some were too bonkers to implement. ("We should clone a bunch of sheep," I suggest. "And open, like, a Dolly petting zoo.")

Zack and I had changed the world—*our* world, anyway—and changed it for the better. The '90s were the most fun time of my life, but I was having even *more* fun by recreating them.

We had the happiest Christmas since we were kids, exchanging gifts from K·B Toys and watching *Home Alone*, *The Muppet Christmas Carol*, *Jack Frost*, *The Grinch* and *The Santa Clause*. (Whenever I hear Mariah Carey's "All I Want for Christmas Is You," I try to ignore memories of Melanie singing it to me during previous holiday seasons.)

The twenty-first century is all about anxiety. When you're not worried about your job security or health insurance premiums, you're worried about factory farming, identity theft, antibiotic resistance, suicide bombers, crazed gunmen, cellphone brain tumors and ruining your reputation with one impulsive tweet. The nonstop insecurity makes you second-guess yourself—and triple-guess your second guesses—until you can't even function.

So getting back in touch with my inner reckless teenager felt thrilling, felt *freeing*. Good times, good times! You only live once? I was alive again. I never wanted to leave this place.

Was it my generation's version of a midlife crisis? Who cares? A massive weight had been lifted from our souls, a stain purged. We had given ourselves the greatest gift of all: a second youth.

It was heaven. And it smelled like teen spirit.

III:
Tragic Kingdom

21.

Even with my Cobain/Nowell hero complex and my recent enjoyment of ecstasy, I never understood why anybody would stick a needle into their veins and inject a potentially lethal substance. So why did I agree to let Evangeline tie a latex strap around my bicep? Because it's difficult to turn down suggestions from a beautiful, unbalanced woman.

"Evie, I'm *really* not sure about this," I say in my hotel room. "What about that guy from Alice in Chains who rotted on his couch for two weeks before police found the body?"

"You won't rot on your couch," Evangeline says. "Not for two weeks."

"I don't want to die, OK, just a little, I don't want to d—"

"Relax, Hind..." She fills the syringe. "You've never felt better."

My heart slams inside my chest as the needle pricks the underside of my forearm. Just as she's about to press the plunger forward, my 1999 Clamshell iBook laptop emits a beep. A new window opens in AOL Instant Messenger. *It's from Melanie.* I breathe a sigh of relief as Evangeline retracts the syringe, but now my heart's slamming even harder.

> **MelanieSavesTheWorld1997 (12:24:35):** Hi, Jake...
>
> **JacobHindsight (12:24:57):** OMG! It's been forever since you logged on AIM.
>
> **MelanieSavesTheWorld1997 (12:25:08):** Ha, yeah, I can't believe it still has my away message with Fiona Apple lyrics.
>
> **JacobHindsight (12:25:11):** What's going on?
>
> **MelanieSavesTheWorld1997 (12:25:23):** You know me...all work, all the time. How's your grand social experiment going?
>
> **JacobHindsight (12:25:30):** Amazingly. This place is SO much fun!!!!
>
> **MelanieSavesTheWorld1997 (12:25:33):** Consider me impressed. :)

JacobHindsight (12:26:04): I still wish you'd come. I miss you...maybe that's awkward to say?

MelanieSavesTheWorld1997 (12:27:01): Not awkward, it's mutual. Glad you haven't replaced me yet with some girl who's as crazy about the '90s as you are.

Glancing at Evangeline across the room, I don't feel a stab of guilt; I feel an evisceration of it.

MelanieSavesTheWorld1997 (12:27:06): Actually, Jake, I wanted to ask...

JacobHindsight (12:27:19): Yeah?

MelanieSavesTheWorld1997 (12:27:42): What would you think about me visiting? I applied for diplomatic clearance, my bosses are cool with it. How about for New Year's Eve?

JacobHindsight (12:27:58): Wow...I'd love for you to STAY, not just visit for a winter vacation...but it'd be great to see you.

MelanieSavesTheWorld1997 (12:28:06): Maybe I need to dip my toe in the water first. <3

I could chat with Mel all day long, but Zack knocks on the door.

"Jacob!" he says. "I need your girlfriend's technical expertise."

He's referring to Evangeline. Not the girlfriend I just invited here.

22.

Zack has rigged up a computer lab on the top floor of City Hall, overlooking the Kurt Cobain statue in the lobby. A 14.4 kbps dial-up modem connects to the Internet with pops and beeps and white-noise static. (I used to hear that cacophonous sound numerous times per day; Mom had to pay for a second landline because I tied up the phone so often.)

"Can you install throwback operating systems—Windows 98, Mac OS 8—as the default for our entire network?" Zack asks Evangeline, pacing across the room and stroking the goatee he's grown; it's the definitive '90s facial hairstyle.

She regards Zack as if he were a mental patient. "I *could*, but I don't follow your logic..."

"If we're using modern technology, we can't have a legitimate '90s experience, yet we lack enough vintage computers for every citizen."

"That old software isn't better, just slower. And whatever nostalgia value can be had from obsolete programs like Netscape Navigator, the security holes alone would—"

"*Everything has to be just the way it was*," Zack bellows. "No Facebook, no Twitter, no Gmail, no Skype...if you want to teleconference, use a Connectix QuickCam."

"Uh, Zack, dude?" I say. "Isn't that a bit extreme?"

Incidentally, this is what I asked him when he banned any non-'90s food, including fresh grains, fruits and vegetables. No meat except for Slim Jims, no dairy except for Kraft Handi-Snacks processed cheese. Malnutrition has already set in, and there's strict rationing because, oops, we're running out of twenty-year-old grub.

"Anything less than *perfect* is a *lie*," Zack says. "A lie is not *authentic*. We are creating 100 percent *authenticity* here, don't you of all people *get* that?"

"Fine, I'll change it now," Evangeline says to calm him down. "But when this gets hacked, just remember: You make the call, you take the fall."

23.

While Evangeline modifies the network, I stroll around the boardwalk, debating my dilemma. As much as I love Mel, she doesn't *get* me—she doesn't get the *'90s*—but I can't expect a healthy, caring, long-term relationship with an anarchic drug addict either, can I?

Despite singing a few verses of "Hakuna Matata," I've still got worries. The Magic Eye Museum, which exhibits framed 3-D optical illusions, makes me feel queasy. I barely manage to hold down the buffalo tenders at Planet Hollywood (still technically operational back in America, but with only a fraction of its '90s locations), as I admire cinematic props and oddities such as the Jaguar XKE from *Austin Powers*, the mask from *Scream* and the weapons—*katana, nunchaku, sai, bo*—from the live-action *Teenage Mutant Ninja Turtles* trilogy.

Back at the hotel, a copy of the *New Yore Times* newspaper, Zack's pride and joy, rests on the doormat, announcing that the reunited Spice Girls, Blur, Oasis and Republica will play a "Cool Britannia" festival on New Year's Eve, which gets me thinking further about Melanie's visit.

Until Evangeline bursts through the door.

"Julian Shango isn't *trying* to build long-range missiles," she says. "He's *got* them."

"Uh..." I say. "Back up?"

"I snooped around San Añorar's military server while upgrading—*down*grading—ours for your nutjob brother. You don't even want to know how Shango persecuted those democratic protesters with our Kickstarter money. A page from Bashar al-Assad's playbook, another page from Augusto Pinochet's... secret police everywhere, torture chambers, death squads, mass graves, *murdered children*, Hind."

I'm not the expert political mind of the family, but I'm pretty sure this is bad. "We should tell Zack."

"Did you hear what I *just said* about 'your nutjob brother'?"

"I know Zack comes across as extreme, but he's rational deep down...well, *strategic*. And he hates dead kids. I mean, he hates it when kids die, you know?"

She sighs. "You make the call..."

"I know, I know...I take the fall."

24.

By SkyWord text message, Zack and I arrange to meet discreetly in the San Añorar Botanical Garden. I convey the nuclear intel that Evangeline digitally dug up.

"So what?" Zack says. "A leader has the right to defend himself and his country from internal and external threats. Frankly, I feel safer knowing that Julian can protect us."

"What if he goads the U.S. into a war?" I ask. "We don't want to get caught in the middle!"

"The American people are sick of war, Jacob. That's why '90s Island *exists*. The real problem here is your easy, sleazy hacker babe rifling through Julian's classified doc—"

Zack stops mid-sentence when he notices a guy reading an Amazon Kindle on a nearby park bench.

"Are you *ignorant* of our rules here..." Zack grabs the device from the guy's hands. "Or perfidiously choosing to *ignore* them?"

"Yo, dawg, give it back," the Kindle owner says. "I was reading Harry Potter! That's from the '90s..."

Zack glances at the grayscale display. "You mean *Harry Potter and the Deathly Hallows* from 2007?" He drops the Kindle to the ground and stomps on it until microcircuits crumble out. "*Sorcerer's Stone* and *Prisoner of Azkaban* only."

"Simmer down, Zack..." I tug at his sleeve. "It's not that big of a deal."

"I was *right*, wasn't I?" Zack brushes my arm away. "About this place? About how great it would be?"

"Yeah, man, of course," I say. "You know how happy I am here."

"Then why not trust me to *keep* it great? To make it even *greater*?"

I want to explain that we can have '90s fun without being '90s fundamentalists, but there's no convincing Zack of anything. He's always had a few loose screws; they're getting looser.

"You're coming with us, worm..." Zack grips the Kindle owner's neck and yanks him off the bench. "Crimes have consequences."

25.

A guard at the palace escorts us to Shango's private office, decorated with revolutionary memorabilia and black-and-white photographs. Even dictators are nostalgic for their glory days.

"You requested an audience..." Shango cuts and lights a cigar. "What can I do for you boys?"

I want to ask him about the nukes and mass graves, but Zack gave me a stern warning.

"Sir, our society is supposed to have *rules*," Zack says, pushing the Kindle owner forward, "but certain citizens—like this hooligan—refuse to obey. How can there be order without adherence? How can there be society at all?"

Shango listens, exhaling dark smoke. "This is what I discovered soon after *la revolución*. I had liberated my people, only to watch them abuse their new freedom with selfish behavior and ungrateful demands. A regular demonstration of strength became necessary."

So fast I don't see it coming, Shango withdraws his golden Beretta and fires it into the prisoner's stomach; the poor bastard topples facedown and exsanguinates on the floor, oozing blood until there's none left, boundless terror and zero comprehension in his eyes.

"Sedition tolerated is sedition successful," Shango says. "Always."

He hands the smoking pistol to Zack. A gift from master to disciple.

26.

"Jesus Christ Jesus Christ Jesus Christ Jesus Christ..."

These are the only two sounds my mouth can form as Zack and I get the hell out of there. I've never seen anyone die before—even from natural causes—and I wasn't prepared to witness an execution. But Zack, the most emotional guy I know, is inexplicably, in*humanly* calm.

"We have to get off this island," I say. "We have to go back home. To our *real* home."

"Because the U.S. government would never kill its own citizens without trial?" Zack sneers. "Look up the *drone program*, Jacob. Every nation in the world enforces its laws. Why should ours be any different?"

"There's a difference between punishing *actual crimes*—theft, murder, that 'social contract' stuff—and reading a *Harry Potter* ebook. Can't you see that?"

"What I see is your commitment wavering. If you're unprepared to recreate the '90s by any means necessary, take a cue from Big Dogs: *lead, follow or get out of the way.*"

27.

"We need to get help," I tell Evangeline at the hotel. "We need to tell the world."

"Your brother had me block every modern communications site, remember?" Evangeline says. "Nobody's checking Geocities or asking Jeeves about us, Hind. We're off the grid."

I could make a phone call or send a Hotmail message—or a fax—but to whom? Who would even care?

Whenever I close my eyes, I see that Kindle owner shuddering with his final breath, unable to make sense of a senseless punishment. And each time it replays, *I* shudder. To escape the looping horror, I beg Evangeline for the only psychic alleviant powerful enough.

I ask her for the heroin. All the heroin. All at once.

There's no nervousness this time, no concern for mortality. White static opiate euphoria fills my world; it feels like swimming inside that 14.4 kbps modem. And it almost feels like peace.

28.

I have no idea how long I've been unconscious.
(Hours? Days? A week?) All I know is I've never felt
so much pain before. The ecstasy hangover was a
joyride in comparison. Every cell in my body is
screaming in torment; I retch and quiver and sob and
endeavor to keep my sanity from disintegrating while
I vomit and vomit and vomit and vomit and vomit on
the queen-size bed.

Evangeline is gone. I look for a note
indicating her whereabouts but find none. Although I
doubt that my stomach can keep food down, however
paltry the ration, I need to eat something. I stagger
out of the room. No one in the hallway, no one in the
elevator, no one in the ground-floor lobby.

Did everybody leave the island? I wonder. *How
could they forget me?*

The boardwalk is a ghost town; I consider the
possibility that I'm experiencing a vivid, heroin-
induced hallucination. And then I hear a faraway
voice booming from the amphitheater.

It's Zack's.

29.

He has gathered each and every '90s Island citizen—
thousands upon thousands—for a compulsory town
hall meeting. Armed guards everywhere, a scene out
of North Korea...or more like hell.

"We all came here for a purpose," Zack
addresses the crowd. "To turn our backs on a world
that had turned its back on us. Some of you, however,
wanted it both ways: one foot in our glorious past, the
other planted in the sick present beyond these shores.
I generously tolerated such fundamental treason
during a transitional period...but no longer."

Guards bring a half-dozen millennials onstage,
in cuffs and chained together.

"The prisoners before you trafficked
hazardous contraband to this sanctuary," Zack
continues. "Post-'90s technology, food, music, film,
litera—"

"I brought *medicine*," explains one of the
detainees. "For life-threatening allergies; my doctor
prescribed it. Why does it matter if the pills went on
the market a couple years ago?"

"Your medicine is not *authentic*," Zack shouts.
"All citizens' quarters, belongings and persons are
now subject to random inspection."

This elicits widespread gasps; Zack fires his golden pistol skyward to silence them.

"The punishment is one year in the Macarena Gulag. A subsequent violation—props to a comely TV anchorwoman—will merit a life sentence in 'Who Let the Dogs Out?' solitary confinement."

He's never mentioned these sadistic disciplinary measures to me. Absolute power corrupts absolutely; my brother was corrupted with a morsel of it.

I feel a buzz in my pocket. A new beeper message from Melanie: "Just arrived for NYE! :)"

30.

"Mel?" I say, dashing toward the pier; *this is the worst possible time.* "It's so great to see you! Welcome to '90s Island!"

I know we're broken up and I'm with Evangeline now—wherever she went—but I throw my arms around Melanie anyway because I'm scared out of my mind. She stiffens with the embrace instead of relaxing. I lean in to kiss her; she turns and I peck her cheek, newly cognizant that she's willing to visit me but not yet willing to forgive me.

"We can start slow," I say. "Why don't I show you around?"

"I'd like that..." She smiles. "Both of those things."

I give Melanie a tour of the hotels, the arcade, the megaplex, the boardwalk and the Botanical Garden, keeping her as far away from the amphitheater barbarity as I can.

"You'll feel at home in no time," I stall, perspiring heavily. "At first *I* was skeptical about whether we could make this idea stick, but now I'd never want to leave. Ha! Ha! Ha!"

"You're acting really weird, Jake," she says. "Aren't there other people here?"

"Yeah, uh, about that..." I take a deep breath. "Oh God, Mel, we're *so* fucked."

31.

I tell her everything—from Shango's nukes to Zack's crackdown—with the exception of Evangeline.

"Jake..." Melanie whispers, pressing her right hand across her left breast. "If you've personally done anything terrible—even if you were following orders—please don't talk about it."

I think she's trying to convey a message, but I'm more concerned that sleeping with Evangeline would count as *anything terrible*. Not admitting the truth makes me feel like a liar, but doing so would hurt Melanie ("*Glad you haven't replaced me yet with some girl who's as crazy about the '90s as you are*") and then I'd just hate myself even more.

In the distance we hear *rat-a-tat-tat*. It's New Year's Eve, but those are definitely machine gun bullets, not fireworks.

"Holy shit," I say, "I think that came from City Hall."

"We need to go there," Melanie says. "Right now."

"Shouldn't we head in the, uh, *opposite* direction?"

"Not if we're on the brink of another Benghazi-level incident." She looks downward as she speaks, projecting her voice toward her clavicle. "Or worse."

"What's a Benghazi?" I ask, but Melanie's already running.

32.

"What do we want? Our iPhones! When do we want them? Now!"

Twenty-somethings wearing Gap cargo khakis, flowered Elaine Benes dresses and other '90s fashions pump their fists and chant in unison. Police with black everything—helmets, shields, nightsticks, jackboots—fire tear gas into the nonviolent crowd and begin cracking bones. It's like the 1999 Seattle WTO riots, except this time Zack is on the side of unrestrained authority.

"Mel...'90s Island isn't *like* this," I say from our vantage point behind a palm tree. "It's *good*, it's *happy*...everything was *magic* until today."

"You know the problem with magic?" Melanie averts her eyes from the carnage. "It's not real."

"Can you ask someone at the State Department for help?"

"I..." She stops herself. "This is way beyond diplomacy now."

"It's one of the fucking Hind brothers," yells a protester whose face is covered with blood, noticing me behind the palm tree trunk. *"Get him! Make him pay!"*

The crowd rushes toward us. I open my mouth to explain that I had nothing to do with the Macarena Gulag—to explain that Melanie just got here, so at least spare her, *please* spare her while ripping me limb from limb—but you can't speak logic to a mob eager for vengeance. A mob convinced of your inhumanity. A mob that only sees guilt and only sees red. A mob rapidly closing in.

Until, that is, police unload a hailstorm of artillery. The protesters go down, one by one, brains and guts splattering on tropical flora; most of their corpses don't even have faces. Yesterday I hadn't seen anyone die...now I've seen an execution *and* a massacre.

"Come with us, Mister Hind," says one of the policemen. "It's not safe for you here."

Was it ever safe for me here on '90s Island? Was it ever safe for anyone?

33.

In the City Hall computer lab, Zack plays *SimCity*—creating an artificial civilization whim by whim, watching from his God's-eye view—as if nothing's happened, as if he carries no responsibility for the bloodbath outside. Snacking on PB Max and Gushers and Kudos, a veritable feast while his people starve, he ignores me and expresses no emotion until Melanie enters the room.

"Why the *fuck* is *she* here?" Zack bolts from his chair, outright loathing on his face. "What is a *spy* doing in our midst?"

"Uh, Zack, it's Mel," I say. "We missed each other, so she came to visit for New Year's."

"She works at the *State Department*, Jacob. Don't you know how the CIA operates through the Foreign Service?"

"The CIA?" I scoff. "Dude, you're so paranoid...she's a policy analyst, not Aeon Flux."

He grips Melanie by the neck—just like he gripped the Kindle owner's—and rips her shirt open; I almost tackle him until I notice the electronic wire taped to her chest.

"She took advantage of you, Jacob, *preyed* on your sentimental vulnerability..." Zack presses the golden Beretta against Melanie's forehead. "A vulnerability to which I'm immune."

"Zack," she says, "I was trying to *protect* y—"

"Stop talking, bitch." Zack cocks the pistol.

I throw myself, reflexively, between them.

"What kind of monster are you becoming?" I ask my brother. "What happened to the guy who cared about social justice? About civil rights? The guy who would've stood with those protesters outside instead of ordering them mowed down?"

"They weren't *pure enough* for this place."

"This place *isn't* pure, Zack. Not anymore."

"We have to make the rules clear—just this once—and then everybody here can have fun again."

"Nobody here will *ever* have fun again. You've traumatized them for life. And if you pull that trigger on Melanie, you'll traumatize me too."

Zack stares me down for a long, hard minute—I fear him more with each passing second—and then lowers the firearm. "Take her to the prison downstairs," he tells a guard. "Consider this a personal favor, Jacob. Our heaven is on earth, but it still requires faith; don't put yours into question."

34.

"So you're really CIA?" I ask Melanie through the shatterproof glass door of her cell; I'd unlock it if only I knew the electronic keypad code. "And you never told me?"

I visited as soon as Zack would allow me. Hours have passed since her detainment; it's a quarter 'til midnight, although you'd never guess, due to the lack of windows down here.

"Of course I'm not..." Melanie sighs. "They determined I could get to you and Zack—talk *sense* to you—easier than any of their agents. It got assessed as an even riskier plan than *Argo*'s...you wouldn't understand that reference; the last Ben Affleck movie you saw was *Armageddon*."

"So you didn't come here to be with me?" I ask, genuinely hurt. "Just to wiretap me?"

"I wanted to keep you *safe*, Jake. You locked yourself inside a nuclear tinderbox—along with thousands of other Americans—and then started playing with matches."

"How was I supposed to know that Zack would go Stalin-level, Mussolini-level crazy?"

"This didn't happen all because of *him*. It was also *you* and your *sickness*, your inability to accept maturity or reality or the slightest responsibility. Even now, are you blind to that?"

"Wow, Hind, you pick all the sweethearts," Evangeline says from the adjacent cell.

"*Evie?*" I feel my heart skip. "This is where you've *been?*"

"Your brother had 'concerns' about whether I'd broadcast the heinous shit I found on Shango's military server," Evangeline says. "Legitimate concerns, but it's still a huge dick move...which I suppose confirms that huge dicks run in your family."

"Excuse me," Melanie says, drawing a deep enough breath to make an Olympic swimmer jealous, "*who* is this?"

"Mel..." The guilt crescendos inside me. "You and I were broken up, so I...um...it wasn't *cheating*, you know? And I thought about you all the time, but you stayed in D.C., so—"

"I should've stayed there *longer*," Melanie mutters. "Why did I try to save you? Why have I spent *years* trying to save you from your own idiocy?"

"I never wanted to hurt you, Mel...plus I was on a *bunch* of ecstasy at the time."

"*Stop talking.* Just go away, all right? Go *away* and take the '90s with you."

35.

Back upstairs, Zack gazes pensively out a window overlooking the turbulent ocean. "The situation has escalated. Julian will return soon. He'll know what to do."

This sounds like manic babbling until I approach the floor-to-ceiling pane; in the distance, on the dark, moonlit horizon, I can make out the shape of a U.S. Navy aircraft carrier.

"Maybe killing demonstrators and jailing a State Department employee wasn't the best idea?" I say. "You know, Zack, on an *island full of WMDs*?"

"A Pentagon shock-and-awe campaign won't intimidate Julian," Zack says. "He survived the Bay of Pequeños in '61, the international missile crisis in '62...he'll survive this."

"I'm more concerned about *us* than him."

"As you should be!" Shango stands in the doorway. A viewscreen descends from the ceiling, displaying a man's craggy, patrician face and coiffed gray hair. He looks presidential; a couple elections back, he almost *was* presidential.

"Do you know who I am, boys?" says the U.S. secretary of state.

"You're...um...Melanie's boss," I say. "Her boss's boss's boss."

"Correct. And I expect her to show up for work on January second."

"You're in the business of making deals," Zack says, "which means you're familiar with the concept of a bargaining chip. If we give her to you, what do you give to us?"

"The USS *Harry S. Truman* is the only bargaining chip in this situation, young man. It's time to surrender. Unlike the civilians you slaughtered today, you'll receive a fair trial by jury."

"The arrogance, the *hypocrisy*," Zack fumes. "Lecturing us on collateral damage and threatening us with a vessel named after the man who killed a *quarter million civilians* in Hiroshima and Nagasaki."

"There's a time for bluster, Zackary," Shango cautions. "And there's a time for realism."

"We have to defend ourselves," Zack says. "That's the reality; they're *coming* for us."

"No, merely for you..." Shango grimaces. "The secretary and I have reached an extradition agreement. In return, he guarantees the curtailment of sanctions against San Añorar."

"What?" Zack's voice is nearly inaudible; he sounds like a kid who's just learned that Santa Claus isn't real. "How could you sell out to Washington? How could you betray your lifelong ideals for *money?*"

"You weren't cut out for leadership, Zackary," Shango says. "You're too temperamental, too inflexible. No man stays in power without a consistent pragmatic streak."

"Liar..." Zack withdraws the golden pistol. *"YOU FUCKING LIAR!"*

My brother doesn't hesitate. In a cloud of smoke and a geyser of blood, Julian Shango—icon of his time—dies at the barrel of his own gun.

"You want us?" Zack says to the secretary of state. "Come get us."

36.

Our wing of the palace is (thank God) isolated enough that no guards hear the shot. Zack snatches Evangeline from her cell and shoves her down at a terminal in the computer lab.

"We know that Shango built nuclear missiles," he says. "Let's see if they fly."

Evangeline's jaw drops as far as mine. "I won't start a war," she says.

Zack jams the Beretta into her mouth. "Oh, I think you'll play along."

I try to shame him into yielding. "What would Mom say if she could see this?"

"She wouldn't say anything, Jacob, because she's *out of her fucking mind*."

"Check a mirror, you lunatic," Evangeline growls, teeth around the gun.

"We are *never* leaving '90s Island," Zack says. "We'll die here one way or another."

"Uh, Zack..." I say. "What exactly does 'one way or another' mean?"

"Time to decide, brother: Are we in this together? Are we family?"

"*Nobody* is with you," I say. "Nobody on this island—on this *planet*—is with you right now."

"You never believed. *None* of you did." Zack forces Evangeline's fingers onto the keyboard. "At midnight, immolate the aircraft carrier. Mar the warhead trajectory, and I'll mar *your* head."

Midnight? I check the clock.

"That's in a *minute*," I say.

"No time like the present."

37.

I race downstairs as fast as I can, *faster* than I can. "We don't have much time, Mel," I say, hyperventilating. "Zack's firing Shango's nukes. If '90s Island can't exist, he doesn't want *anything* to exist. Christ, I'm so sorry."

Absorbing this, Melanie looks away from me and toward the corner of her cell. "You don't have to say you're sorry, Jake. I'd rather die in silence."

"No, I...I need to say this. Because I have a lot of regrets—so many, *too* many—but the biggest is that I forgot to cherish our time together, every second of it, every *new* second. Even if we only have a few left, I want to make them count. And they will, as long as I'm with you."

My words hang in the air. Melanie places a hand on the glass door; I place mine on the other side. "That's all I ever wanted to hear," she says, tears welling in her eyes.

Ten.

"Mel, I love you."

Five.

"I love you forever."

Three.

"*Now* and forever."

Two. One. Midnight.

All the power goes out.

38.

Without electricity, the door clicks unlocked. *It can't be that simple*, I think. *Shango wouldn't let prisoners go free because of a little power outage.*

Whatever the answer, Melanie and I make a run for it, feeling our way through the darkness. The backup generators kick in as we reach City Hall's lobby. And that's when Evangeline falls headfirst from the top floor, her hands bound with some kind of...*nunchuks?*

The crack. We hear Evangeline's skeleton *crack.*

"Oh Jesus." I kneel beside her twisted, broken body. "Please be alive, please be al—"

"Windows...98..." She flashes a crimson smile of pyrrhic triumph. "No...Y2K patches."

Suddenly I understand her hacker masterstroke: *It's New Year's Day 2000, and the millennium bug—which humanity spent $500 billion to contain—has just struck San Añorar.*

"You're a genius, Evie," I say. "A *genius.*"

"You just saved all of us," Melanie says.

"Authenticity..." Evangeline coughs blood; her voice is so faint. "That's his weakness, that's how..." She struggles to keep her eyes open. "Hind, I...hope you had...the time of your..."

A final puff of air escapes her lungs. Silence.

"Life," I finish her sentence, right before three blades pierce my back.

"*Death*," Zack says, removing the *sai*; he's strapped the Ninja Turtles movie trilogy weapons from Planet Hollywood to his body. "Cowabunga!"

Zack slams Donatello's *bo* into my sternum. The blow sends me airborne toward the Kurt Cobain statue; the glass case housing our guitar bursts into a thousand shards upon impact.

"*Jake*," Melanie screams. "He's trying to *kill you*."

"That's right, bitch, my brother is going to die, and it's all your fault." Zack unsheathes Leonardo's *katana*. "If you hadn't come to destroy this place, he'd still be alive, still be *happy*."

"You don't get it, Zack..." I crawl backwards, a trail of blood streaking the floor. "*She* makes me happy."

"I'll always remember the times we shared, Jacob." Zack raises the blade over my cranium. "Times we could've shared a *second* time, if you'd only believed."

The SkyWord pager falls out of my pocket. Before Zack realizes it, Melanie—who returns my nod, because we speak a language deeper than words—whips out her smartphone and hits the speed-dial key. A discordant, ear-splitting squawk distracts him for the slightest of moments. I grab Kurt Cobain's guitar—my most treasured possession, the physical epitome of my long-idealized youth—and break it over Zack's skull with concussive force.

"See?" I say to Melanie. "Pagers *are* practical!"

"An iPhone just saved your life," Melanie says.

"All right, all right, add me to your service plan." We see far-off fireworks and hear the Spice Girls. "Happy New Year, Mel. You complete me."

She actually laughs at the *Jerry Maguire* reference. "Since when are you happy that time is moving forward?"

"Since I learned forward is the only direction it *can* move."

"You know all the right things to say to your girlfriend today."

"'Girlfriend'?" I smile from ear to ear. "Booyah! Do I make you horny? Randy? Do I make you *horny*, baby, yeah, do I? Wassssssssssssssssssssup?"

"Talk to the hand, Jake." She kisses me, and it feels like home. All the nostalgia I need—all that I've *ever* needed—is right here in my arms.

IV:
Unplugged

39

After boarding the aircraft carrier, all '90s Island residents were repatriated as citizens in good standing. Zack's trial for crimes against humanity is set for next summer; Melanie pulled some major strings—the administration owed her a favor—and I'm testifying in exchange for immunity. (I'd feel like a snitch, but...y'know...he did try to kill me with a *katana*.)

With Shango dead, San Añorar is preparing to hold its first democratic election since the mid-twentieth century. The people were living in slums and shanties while we luxuriated in high-rises, ignorant of their suffering. Sanctions dropped, their economy is rebounding.

Just like our own economy. The Dow Jones is at an all-time high. Jobs are coming back by the hundreds of thousands. Georgetown Gutter finally closed for good, but I'm now a music recommendation specialist at Spotify, the subscription-based audio streaming app that all the kids love these days. I have to admit, it's more convenient than CDs.

I donated my old toys, clothes and games to charity. When Microsoft updated my Hotmail address to Outlook.com, I didn't even mind; it looks more adult anyway.

My bank account, miracle of miracles, gets flusher—not flushed—with each subsequent month, but my self-worth isn't rising as fast as my net worth. Like most guys, I'm not comfortable talking about emotional damage. You go to war, lose a limb or four, and keep on keepin' on. You survive. You deal. You ignore the psychic fallout. You suffer in silence. You pretend it never happened.

When the global financial system crashed in October 2008, however, we *all* got damaged. Our sense of stability vanished along with our faith in the future. Since then it's been anxiety and entropy and existential panic; our formative years were defined by deformation.

If you kept your job, you had to work quadruple the hours—under a permanent threat of *never enough*—because somebody, somewhere, would work *quintuple* the hours. If you got downsized, you had to compete with millions of others for worthless scraps. Megacorporations slashed pensions and benefits, replacing the traditional career ladder with unpaid internships, a modern slavery. Too scared to protest, too eager to please, we accepted it as the new normal.

My face has more creases than it should at my age. Now that I have health insurance again, my doctor found a murmur while listening to my heartbeat. I try to banish the thought, but can't help wondering: *How many years did the stress take off my life? Five? Ten? More?*

Even though I'm earning a decent paycheck, enough to buy Melanie a ring without selling my non-vital organs, I squeeze every last drop out of the ketchup bottle, my grandfather's habit from the Great Depression. I put every spare dime into the rainy-day fund because I won't—*can't*—trust sunny days. This isn't fiscal prudence; it's economic PTSD.

My original trauma, however, occurred long ago. And only one thing could heal it.

40.

Melanie and I take a road trip out to California. With all the flower murals, beaded vests, bell-bottoms and patchouli, you'd swear my father's commune was a portal to 1969. He's grayer and thinner than I expect—almost *withered*—and he doesn't recognize me.

"What's happenin', my man?" Dad asks when I approach. "Groovy weather, huh?"

"Sir..." I feel every human emotion at once. "My name is Jake Hind...I'm your son."

"The tarot cards predicted a special visitor." He extends a leathery hand; I'm unsure whether to shake it or wring his neck for abandoning me. "Is your brother here too?"

"We'll have time to talk about him, but first I need to tell you something..." I'm shaking as I speak; Melanie squeezes my arm for support. "I understand, all right? I understand why you did it—why you left— and that doesn't mean I forgive you, but I also don't blame you anymore. Because your flaws are my flaws, and you didn't ask for them any more than I did."

"Thank you, Jake, that's a beautiful sentiment...I can't say I felt proud, and I've wanted to get in touch with you for so long, but staying out of your life seemed less cruel than intruding."

"Maybe you're right," I say. "You're coming back with me, though."

"Coming back?" He laughs. "This is my home; I'm happy here."

"No, Dad, you *think* you're happy, but you're not. And besides, you missed my childhood; I'm not gonna let you miss my wedding."

"Ah, I see..." Dad smiles at Melanie. "You must make my son very happy. Well, I'd love to attend."

"There's just one condition if you want to be part of my life...part of *our* lives," I say. "You have to help Mom. She can't remember much. Not me, not Zack—which is probably for the best—but she remembers *you*, and she's so alone, and she misses you so, so much."

"That's..." He lowers his head in shame, a shame I never knew he had. "Yes, I can help."

I put a hand on his shoulder and slide in for the hug, and I cry like a baby in his arms because I love him and I hate him at the same time, but I think I can learn to just love him.

"I've got one condition too," Dad says.

"Yeah?" I wipe away snot. "Name it."

"We're taking my ride out of here."

I have no idea *how* the Volkswagen bus still works—German engineering?—but it cruises onto Highway 1 at twenty over the speed limit. Our conversation gets easier with each passing mile of coastline. As the hours go by, it dawns on me: *This is what family feels like.*

Those who forget the past are doomed to repeat it; so are those who forget the present. The '90s were an objectively better time—that's not just a halcyon myth—but even though we're living in harder times now, *we still have to* live *in them.* Will I always look back with fondness at my yesterdays? Sure...but mostly I'm looking forward to my tomorrows.

On KROQ-FM, the opening strings of Blink-182's "What's My Age Again?" play, but I turn the radio off before the chorus and power chords kick in.

"Jake!" Melanie says. "It was just getting to the good part."

"Shouldn't I listen to new bands? Get with the times?"

"A great song is a great song—whenever it's from."

I turn the music back on. It sounds better than ever.

About the Author

Marty Beckerman is also the author of #1 Amazon.com best-selling parody *The Heming Way* (St. Martin's Press). He has written for the *New York Times*, the *Atlantic*, *Esquire*, *Playboy*, *Maxim*, *Wired*, *Mental Floss*, *Nerve*, *Salon*, *Discover*, the *Daily Beast* and MTV. He lives in New York and had frosted tips until 2002.